HURRAY FOR CAPTAIN JANE!

Hurray For Captain Jane!

Story by Sam Reavin

Pictures by Emily Arnold McCully

Parents' Magazine Press • New York

*

To One Magnificent Woman

Jane went to a party and came home with three packages.

Her little brother, Simon, met her at the door.

"What's in all those packages?" he asked.

"Prizes," Jane said. She looked very proud. "I won them at the party."

"Open them, open them!" said Simon. "Let's see what's inside."

Jane opened the littlest package first. It was a box of jelly beans.

"Can I have all the black ones?" asked Simon.

"No," Jane said. "I like the black ones, too."

She opened the biggest package next and took out a hat made of folded wax paper.

"A sailor's hat!" said Simon. "Can I have it?"

"No," Jane said. "It's mine!" And she put it on.

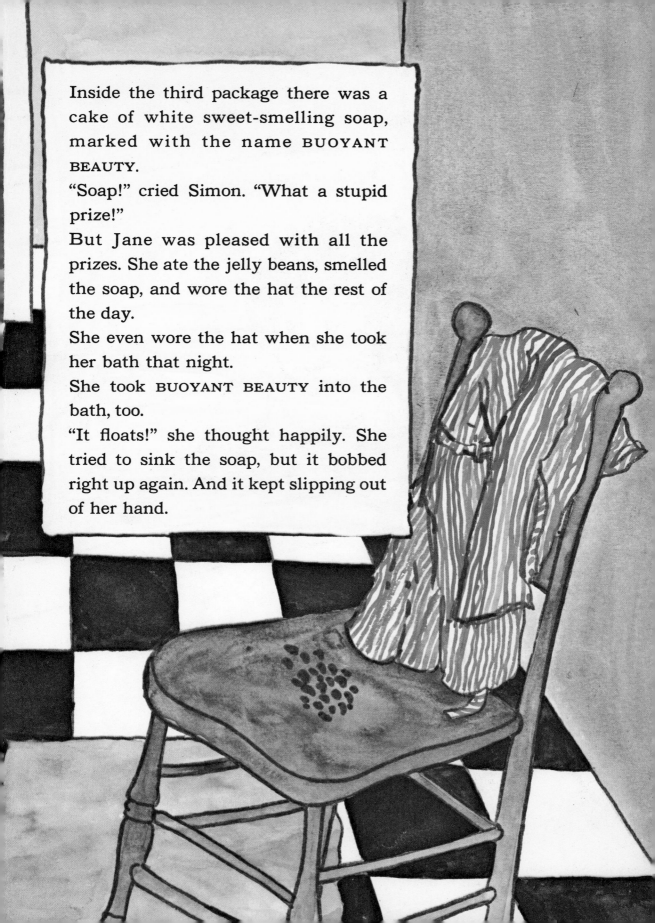

Inside the third package there was a cake of white sweet-smelling soap, marked with the name BUOYANT BEAUTY.

"Soap!" cried Simon. "What a stupid prize!"

But Jane was pleased with all the prizes. She ate the jelly beans, smelled the soap, and wore the hat the rest of the day.

She even wore the hat when she took her bath that night.

She took BUOYANT BEAUTY into the bath, too.

"It floats!" she thought happily. She tried to sink the soap, but it bobbed right up again. And it kept slipping out of her hand.

She leaned over to grab BUOYANT BEAUTY, and her hat fell into the water. She was about to put it on again when she saw that the hat floated like a little ship. She could make it go, too. When she stirred the water with her hands, the ship seemed to sail at her command.

"I can make it go faster," Jane said. She sank into the tub until the water came up to her chin. Then she kicked her feet and made little waves. The ship began to sail toward her—faster and faster. As it came closer and closer, it looked bigger and bigger.

Bump! It touched her chin.

Suddenly the water in the tub became a great ocean.

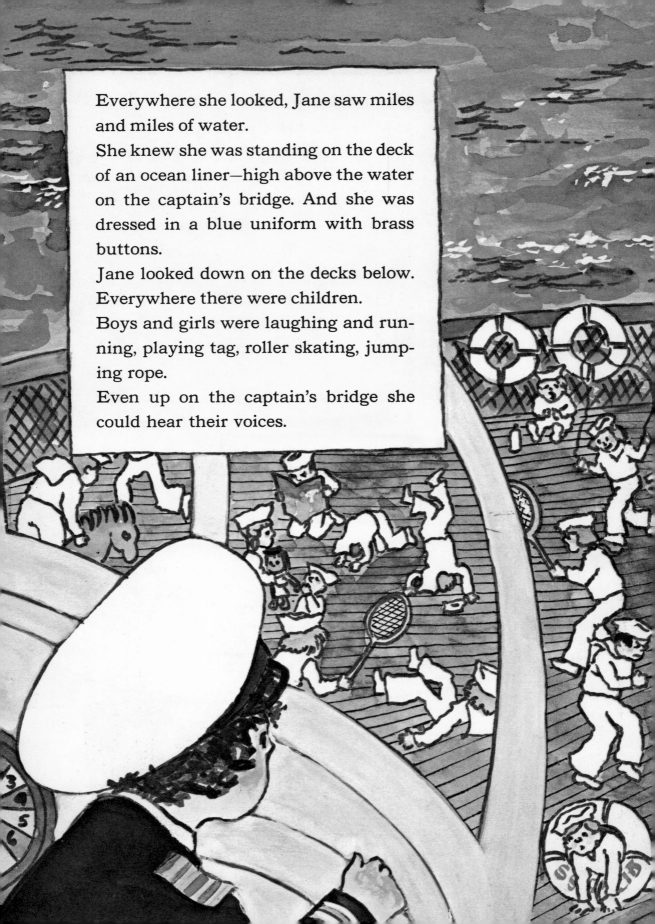

Everywhere she looked, Jane saw miles and miles of water.

She knew she was standing on the deck of an ocean liner—high above the water on the captain's bridge. And she was dressed in a blue uniform with brass buttons.

Jane looked down on the decks below. Everywhere there were children.

Boys and girls were laughing and running, playing tag, roller skating, jumping rope.

Even up on the captain's bridge she could hear their voices.

A girl in a sailor's uniform was on duty at the helm. Jane was glad there was someone to talk to.

"What's your name?" she asked the girl at the wheel.

"Kate, Seawoman First Class," the girl replied.

"My name is Jane."

"Aye, aye, Captain," said Kate, Seawoman First Class.

Captain! Jane looked around. "Oh, I'm the captain of this ship. I'd better get busy."

She pressed a button on her desk.

Almost at once a sailor appeared. He looked just like her brother Simon. He saluted smartly and stood at attention.

"At your service, Captain," he said.

After some thought, Jane said, "Please bring me some black jelly beans."

"Aye, aye, Captain," said the sailor. "Black jelly beans. At once!"

When he returned, Jane said, "Ask the first mate to come to the bridge."

The first mate arrived promptly.

"Please stand watch here," Jane ordered. "I wish to inspect my ship. First I'll check the barometers, the thermometers and the speedometers, then the radarscopes, the telescopes and the thermoscopes."

Jane started her inspection below the main deck, in the engine room. The boys and girls who operated the ship's machinery saluted her as she passed by.

As she went from deck to deck, the children gathered around her. She gave them all black jelly beans.

"Captain," said one of the children, "may I take your picture?"

"Well ..." said Jane, "I'm busy right now."

"Please!" said the boy. "I'd like to have a picture of the first lady captain of an ocean liner."

While he was taking her picture, there was a call on the loudspeaker: "Captain! You are needed on the bridge!"

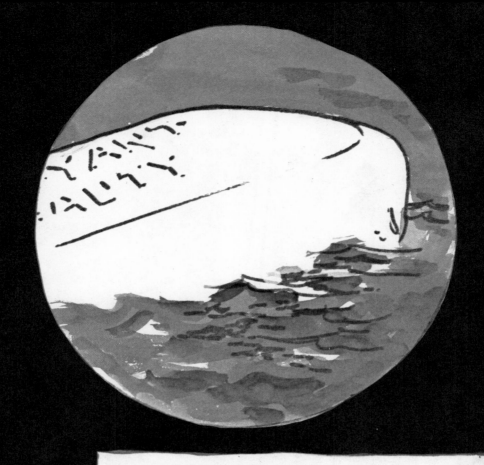

Jane rushed back to the bridge. The first mate was scanning the horizon with his spyglass. He looked worried.

"Captain," he said, "there is an iceberg dead ahead."

Jane picked up a spyglass and studied the iceberg. It looked familiar to her.

"It's almost as big as our ship!" cried the first mate. "And we're heading right for it! Don't you want to change course, Captain?"

Through the glass, Jane could see some letters on the iceberg.

"No," she said coolly. "Stay on course. I want to get a closer look."

Suddenly the children on the decks below grew very quiet.

They stopped running and playing, and stood waiting.

"There's an iceberg ahead," they whispered.

The ship was moving closer and closer to the iceberg. Soon Jane could read the words BUOYANT BEAUTY.

She gave a strange order. "Ready the fire hoses!"

"Ready all fire hoses!" repeated the first mate over the loud-speaker.

"Cut the engines!" Jane ordered.

The engines stopped and the ship began to slow down.

They were almost upon the iceberg and it seemed impossible now to avoid a collision.

"Hose the iceberg!" was Jane's next order.

All the hoses on the great liner were turned on the iceberg.

Powerful streams of water shot out.

To the amazement of everyone but Jane, the iceberg began to melt and drift to the side.

At the same time, clouds of giant bubbles rose into the air—hundreds and hundreds of great bright colored bubbles.

They were out of danger!

"Full speed ahead!" Jane ordered.
As the ship moved forward, the bubbles
floated onto the decks.
Sparkling and spinning, they came
down like a rainfall of balloons.
The children began to chase the big
bubbles. They laughed and shouted as
they tossed them with their hands,
bounced them on their heads, and
threw them to one another.
"Hurray for Captain Jane!" they cried.
"Hurray!"

Jane smiled to herself as she heard the cheering. But it was time to look at the instruments again. "Now I must check the barograph, the thermograph and the graphograph," she said. She was pleased that everything was in order.

"I like to run a tight ship," she told the first mate. Then she noticed that right beside the graphograph there was a shiny brass handle she had not seen before.

"What's this?" she said, and she turned the handle to the right.

There was a loud gurgling sound, and the ocean disappeared.

Jane found herself sitting in an empty tub. Beside her was the cake of soap—now only a thin sliver—and the wax paper hat.

Jane tried to put the hat on, but it unfolded in her hands.

She wanted to fold it back into a sailor's hat again. But no matter how she tried, she could not fold it into the shape it had been.

Instead, the hat looked just like a pilot's cap.

"Oh," said Jane, "maybe next time I'll be the captain of a jet plane."

SAM REAVIN was until his retirement a successful poultry farmer in Kerhonkson, New York, although he had always had a desire to write. He still lives in Kerhonkson with his wife, well-known children's author, Lilian Moore. And it was with her encouragement that Mr. Reavin at last began writing the stories that had been developing in his mind for many years. In addition to *Hurray for Captain Jane!* he will soon publish *Here Come the Hunters!* and *I Wish I Had a Pony*.

EMILY ARNOLD McCULLY was awarded a gold medal by the Philadelphia Art Directors Club in 1968. She has illustrated many books for children including *Maxie* and *The Mouse and the Elephant,* both published by Parents' Magazine Press. Mrs. McCully was born in Illinois. A graduate of Pembroke College of Brown University, she received her M.A. in Art History at Columbia. She now makes her home in Garden City, Long Island, with her husband and two young children.